T0246435

ALSO BY ANITA DESAI

Cry, the Peacock

Voices in the City

Bye-Bye, Blackbird

Where Shall We Go This Summer?

Fire on the Mountain

Games at Twilight

Clear Light of Day

The Village by the Sea

In Custody

Baumgartner's Bombay

Journey to Ithaca

Fasting, Feasting

Diamond Dust

The Zigzag Way

The Artist of Disappearance

The Complete Stories

Rosarita

ANITA DESAI

SCRIBNER

New York Amsterdam/Antwerp London Toronto Sydney New Delhi

Scribner
An Imprint of Simon & Schuster, LLC
1230 Avenue of the Americas
New York, NY 10020

Copyright © 2024 by Anita Desai
Originally published in Great Britain in 2024 by Picador,
an imprint of Pan Macmillan

First Scribner hardcover edition January 2025

SCRIBNER and design are trademarks of Simon & Schuster, LLC

For information about special discounts for bulk purchases, please contact Simon & Schuster Special Sales at 1-866-506-1949 or business@simonandschuster.com.

The Simon & Schuster Speakers Bureau can bring authors to your live event. For more information or to book an event, contact the Simon & Schuster Speakers Bureau at 1-866-248-3049 or visit our website at www.simonspeakers.com.

Manufactured in the United States of America

1   3   5   7   9   10   8   6   4   2

Library of Congress Cataloging-in-Publication Data has been applied for.

ISBN 978-1-6680-8243-0
ISBN 978-1-6680-8245-4 (ebook)

To the memory of my parents

Toni Nimé and Dhirendra Nath Mazumdar

I'M SORRY I DON'T RESPOND
"Each of us is many persons.
To me I'm who I think I am,
        But others see me differently
        And are equally mistaken.

"Don't dream me into someone else
But leave me alone, in peace!
If I don't want to find myself
Should I want others to find me?"

Fernando Pessoa
SONGBOOK (1930)

"an impossible greeting, like one who waves vainly from
one bank of the river to the other knowing there are
no banks, really, believe me, there are no banks, there
is only the river . . . what idiots, we worried so much
about the banks and instead there was only the river."

Antonio Tabucchi
IT'S GETTING LATER ALL THE TIME

ROSARITA

I

All the benches in the Jardín facing the pink spikes and spires of the Parroquia are already taken by lovers of the morning sun, but you find one set back under the meticulously trimmed and shaped trees you are told are Indian laurels, where you can sit making your way at leisure through the Spanish-language newspapers you have bought from the vendor who spreads out a variety of them on the low wall that surrounds the Jardín. Undisturbed except for the distractions provided by the children playing around the bandstand, a balloon seller wandering around in search of a customer and the pigeons strutting the paving stones, bowing to each other and muttering greetings like old gentlemen on their morning constitutionals.

Then becoming aware, without wanting to, of a woman seated on a bench across from you, dressed in the flamboyant Mexican style that few Mexican women assume at any other than festive occasions: skirt upon skirt of cotton and tulle in indigo, lime, crimson and saffron, her arms spread over the back of the bench festooned with bangles. Staring at you fixedly, taking in every detail of your person, it seems, with her deep kohl-rimmed eyes, and it is making you uneasy to be the focus of such unembarrassed attention, acting like insects on your skin, exploring.

Suddenly, as if she can no longer restrain herself, rising in a flurry of scarves and skirts, she almost flings her person and drenching aroma of catechu on you, and there is nothing hesitant or tentative any more. 'Yes,' she declares in a husky purr, 'I *have* been watching you, my darling. I wanted to be very, very sure I was right, and now I am. *Of course* you are, you *must* be, my adored Rosarita's little girl. You are the image of her when she first came to us, an Oriental bird!'

Drawing back and keeping hold of the newspaper as some flimsy form of defence, you say, 'Rosarita – who?'

'But you have her looks, her manner – what to say, her comportment. The mouth, the eyes. You cannot not be my dearest amiga's daughter!'

Putting your feet together in their dusty sandals and

preparing to make an escape from this woman who is altogether too insistent, too intrusive, you say, 'My mother? Her name was Sarita.'

'Did I not say? Did I not see? and *your* name, my *niña*?'

You confess, reluctantly, that your name is Bonita, aware now that in Spanish it sounds more like a childish endearment than a proper name, so you try to explain: 'Like Sunita, Vanita, Ronita . . . common names in India,' but the woman bursts into laughter, exposing many large and discoloured teeth, and closes her eyes as at a delicious joke.

'No, that is *too* beautiful! She would of course have given you a name she heard here!'

'I was named by my father's mother,' you say stiffly, although that is probably untrue and certainly unverifiable. What made you think that up? What made you so defensive? You have come to San Miguel to attend the language school, you should want – and are certainly in need of – exactly such an 'interchange' with a 'native speaker' who approaches you so warmly, so effusively; what makes you draw back and close up?

Her intensity, the floodlight focus of her enormous, theatrically outlined eyes, her ferocious attention. She is not a seller of bangles and bracelets, of scarves and dolls;

she is pursuing you not to sell but to offer – just the exchange you need. And that you now find you don't at all want.

You draw back – in fear, unease or suspicion? Yes, all three. Why, of all approaches, has this stranger in a strange place brought up your mother? An ordinary exchange at a chance meeting this is not. Nor is it one you prepared for with your standard dictionary and helpful phrase book. It makes you press your sandals together and wish you could draw your dark glasses out of your bag so as to screen yourself from her and hide. But hide from whom – this stranger or your mother?

Seeing you sink back, the woman tries again, lowering her voice to a pacifying coo. 'But, my darling, I am Vicky. Vicky, you know, your mother will have told you about me – Victoria? What friends we were? What times we had together?'

'Ehh, no,' you stutter. Mother never mentioned a friend named Victoria in any part of her life, most certainly not in a small town in Mexico. How, when, why would she ever have ventured into this foreign land, met this foreign woman? Or, perhaps, 'In India?' you wonder aloud.

'In India?' The woman bursts into hoarse laughter that makes the pigeons at her feet take off and seek shelter in the trees, where they perch muttering in alarm and indignation. 'In India – *how*? No, no, my darling, right here, where we are sitting, in the Jardín before the Parroquia – right *here*!'

'But *when*?' staying stubborn, resistant.

'When she was your age and looked exactly as *you* do, so I could re-cog-nize you in-stant-ly!'

There is nothing for it – you have to move to one of the cafés in the arcades around the Jardín. 'We must have a coffee together. We cannot part after such a tre-men-dous meeting, can we?'

Tremendous? Or crazy? Based on mistaken identity, surely. Your mother never lived in San Miguel, never even visited Mexico. You know that – the absurdity of such a suggestion! You could tell this woman a thing or two about her. But she insists she knows otherwise. Over the little metal table with its paper-napkin holder and posy of dried and dyed country flowers and tall glasses of iced coffee, she insists while you resist.

You hope for some distraction, look to the old woman who comes by with her basket of little cloth dolls with black string plaits and striped aprons, but the Stranger dismisses her with a wave of her impressively beringed hand, as she does the man in white pyjamas who comes by with fierce lion masks of red and yellow, blue and purple raffia and the children with running noses who hold out trays with tiny packets of Chiclets. Your companion does not allow you to engage with them or their wares and anyway you too pay them little attention, involved against your will in the story being told you. You shake your head over and over again, not given the chance to protest verbally.

Rosarita – as the Stranger urges you to call this mythical mother – Rosarita had come to paint in San Miguel. Did not many come to pursue that art here where there were world-famous art schools, celebrated maestros? Vicky had come across her in the Jardín, painting under the guidance of the maestro Francisco, and seen at once that he gave her more attention than he gave to any other in that group of students. And she, Vicky, watched the young woman's talent unfolding – as well as something else besides talent.

'Besides talent?'

'Yes, yes, her – how to say it? – her *flowering*. So timid, so shy, no confidence at all. Then beginning to smile, her eyes to shine – right here, in the sun, in front of the Parroquia. And I knew Maestro Francisco. One day we were having a drink – here, right here! – and I asked him, who is this new student of yours, where has she come from? And he told me – India!' The Stranger clasps her hands together as if reliving the wonder of that revelation. 'India, he said. I could not believe. All my life I had a longing to visit that country, see its art, learn its language – Sanskrit! I was obsessed. I thought, such an ancient language of the East – I would learn it from a guru – is that right? Once I even wrote to the university in Benares, I thought in that holy city I would find someone to teach me. But they wrote back that they did not accept women. Ahh, I was crushed, destroyed, so disappointed was I. How could it be I would not be allowed to come and learn? And now here was this young creature who had come all the way to *my* country, to study art in *my* land. I knew we were *meant* to meet!'

The woman's speech is a torrent, unstoppable. She allows no interruption, no protest, the protest you are struggling to make. You ought to say, bluntly, she is mistaken, your mother did not paint, not in India and not in Mexico, it must be someone else the Stranger met and remembered. But all you are able to say is, 'I didn't know—'

'But, darling, I see her so clearly before me, as clearly as I see *you*. And you have the same way of putting your fingers to your lips when you speak, pushing your hair back behind your ears, even that charming mole near your mouth. And now you have come to see where she had once been, perhaps also to paint? You are artist too?' She stretches her arm, scrawny and sunburnt, across the table-top as if to reach out and touch you, clutch at this memory she has of someone who did not exist. You shrink from those eyes of hers, so brilliant – do they owe that to the kohl she has used so lavishly? or do you detect a flicker in them of something unidentifiable, like a fish darting out of the undersea into the light?

So you shake your head more determinedly. You do not paint and nor did your mother. The mole on her cheek, her gestures – accurately observed but they do not make a whole person, a personal identity. 'I am a language student. I do not paint, nor did my mother.'

'Ah, no.' She withdraws her outstretched hand, lets it fall onto her lap. She might have been an actress, her gestures are so theatrical. 'Don't tell me she gave up painting. She had *talent*. Francisco saw that, wanted to help it to flower. And you say she gave up on returning to India? But why?'

'I don't know' is all you can think to say.

'A tragedy!' wails the Stranger, and pouts with disappointment. 'She should have stayed *here*, with *us*.'

Now you feel a stir of regret as the Stranger's initial joy at meeting you collapses in this – this so-called tragedy. And in truth you too feel a shadow fall at this, this loss of which you had till now been ignorant. And now that you try to give credence to a past that had never been mentioned or guessed at, that she might once have had and then was withheld, or lost. Was it the loss of what the Stranger is insisting had once existed elsewhere and even 'flowered'?

It is baffling, hard to conjure up and believe in here in this great abundance of light that makes the leaves of the laurel trees shimmer, the pigeons murmur and coo in an expression of mounting ecstasy, figures drift across the Jardín at a pace that is all leisure, all enjoyment; and you pick up your bag, pay for the coffee and say you must leave, you will be expected back at the boarding house where you are staying.

The Stranger recovers from her sadness and becomes immediately animated. She wants to know where it is and nods, taking in the location with an almost audible click.

Making your way back to it, you cannot rid yourself of the suspicion that you are being followed. You do not wish to turn around and catch her at it, but when you reach the door set in the stone wall of your residence and let yourself in, a quick glance over your shoulder shows that you were right: the figure that steps nimbly into a shadowy doorway further up the road is unmistakably draped with skirts and scarves like a gypsy and recognizably the Stranger now turned pursuer.

The walled courtyard has withdrawn into its afternoon siesta: the dining room is empty, the table set for the next meal with plates turned upside down, the other residents out on their own pursuits, empty rooms being cleaned by maids who go in and out with armfuls of laundry, too busy to do more than smile at you as you retreat past the stone fountain chuckling quietly to itself, to your own room at the far end where an archway with a jungle of creepers opens into the garden beyond.

There you dispose of your bag and your sandals and stretch out on the narrow bed spread with thick white cotton sheets and allow yourself to succumb to the lingering fatigue of the long journey that has brought you here. You place your arm across your eyes to shut out the brightness of the window so that you can look instead into the shadows of an interior and shelter there from the cracks that have been revealed by the encounter with the Stranger.

Mother, an artist? In the home you remember as without a paintbrush, a chalk or a sketchbook to be seen?

You recall, though – and it is the very shadows that

come together in brushlike strokes to form it – a sketch in wishy-washy pale pastels that had hung on the wall above your bed at home, of a woman seated on a park bench – and yes, it could have been one here in San Miguel – with a child playing in the sand at her feet. She is not looking at the child and the child is not looking at her, as if they had no relation to each other, each absorbed in a separate world, and silent.

The sketch in its faded rose-pinks and lavenders had become so familiar to you throughout your childhood you had never scrutinized it and it had never occurred to you to ask who had made it, when or where: it was just there.

Now, in the gauzy net of a noontime doze, you strain to remember its particulars, but all that comes through is the afternoon sounds outside, no louder, no more intrusive than the murmur of bees – the gardener sweeping dead leaves off the paving stones with his long twig broom, the ever-present doves gossiping convivially in the trees, a tap running into a tank that collects water – the afternoon unfolding like a scroll, its beginning and its end both invisible.

The scene that should be so foreign to you is, at its deepest level, utterly familiar. You are back in the garden in India that you had known in your earliest years, the years no one mentioned again once they were over, the time when Mother was absent and you were taken to live in your grandparents' house in Old Delhi.

Grandfather could not have been pleased. He clearly believed children ought neither to be seen nor heard. (Father had, you knew, been sent to boarding school at the age of three and a half years, the earliest they would take children.) They were a disturbance to his routine of receiving clients either in his crepuscular office room or seated at an immense desk on the veranda outside it, where he also dictated letters to the clerk who rode up on his bicycle in the afternoons to deal with files and mail. Cups of tea were sent at regular intervals and you were under strict orders to keep to the other side of the house.

This, in any case, was what you preferred. On the other side there stretched out the vegetable garden, neatly divided into squares for the different varieties grown there – cauliflowers in one, each of the great white bouquets covered with a leaf of the plant to act as an umbrella from the sun, while aubergines, chillies and tomatoes grew in other beds in the full sun, and narrow channels for water to run through according to the gardener's calculation of when and where it was required. And although he played at being fierce – twisting his long black, oiled moustache and yelling if he saw you reach out to pluck a cape goose-berry, strip it of its crackling coat and pop it into your mouth, and threatened you with dire punishment, you understood this to be harmless play-acting and his way of paying you attention. That attention was as hard to come by as a gooseberry.

He was also the keeper of the family's dog who, unlike you, was not allowed in the house at all but kept chained to a post outside the gardener's hut. A large, hulking German Shepherd, but one whose spirit had been suc-cessfully crushed by his captivity, he drooped till the hour came when the gardener picked up the chain attached to his collar in one hand and a cudgel-like walking stick in the other and took him out onto the street for a stately promenade as far as a small, dusty park at the end of the road where other dog minders gathered to sit smoking their biris, and back, then fell into his habitual drooping posture outside the hut once again. At last he was brought a tin basin full of bones to gnaw. He was called Sultan and never was a dog more inappropriately named. You were forbidden to touch him and you only looked at each other, covertly, under lowered lids, neither allowed to reach out to the other.

This was the 'other side' of the house, out of Grand-father's jurisdiction and under Grandmother's more benign rule. She herself represented Grandfather's past: he had married her when she was a girl from the same rural dis-trict where he had been born but had left to make his career and his fortune and his name, taken along as the designated appurtenance. It was the role she had been handed to play by her horoscope and that she had taken on and eventually made her own, the matriarch of her own appointed territory. When she was old and experienced enough, and guests complimented her on the meals served at her table, the well-trained servants who served them and the absence of household crises common elsewhere – and the material of much of the social chatter – she would boast of having 'set her household on wheels' and letting it run by itself.

What you remembered of her: how she would sit on a cane stool on the patio outside the kitchen and supervise the making of pickles for which she was famed, having her maids slice green mangoes into slivers, weighing out the spices and measuring the oil that was poured over them in brown-and-white-striped ceramic jars of various sizes. And once that had been done the jars would be lined up along the low wall around the patio and Grandmother would inspect them daily with a look of both achievement and encouragement, give each a pat and a turn towards the sun, occasionally lifting the lids of what would be produced not only on her table but sent around as gifts to favoured relatives and friends.

And as a woman, silver-haired, smelling of coconut hair oil and floral talcum powder after her bath, dressed in either a grey or a beige sari, going out with a tray of sweets and flowers to offer at a small altar of whitewashed bricks that she had had built under the temple tree outside the kitchen. You had been allowed to pick the flowers, long-tongued red hibiscus and cool fragrant jasmine freshly plucked from the hedge, to offer to her favoured god. At the end of the ritual, Grandmother would tuck a small portion of a milky sweet into your open mouth. No one else in the household participated, most certainly not Grandfather, who pretended no altar existed on his property, and certainly no heathen image. If there was a god, it could only be The Husband.

Eventually someone came – Mother or possibly Father – to collect you and transport you – by car, train, plane? you forget – to the next stage of your family life in a modern flat in a modern block in a modern new development of the new city, the old city left to its dusty past. The flat in that block in the development belonged to the company for which Father worked and that kept alive, as long as it could, the 'boxwallah' tradition of trade after the British themselves withdrew and their empire became untenable and unmentionable. The inhabitants of that block were expected to maintain their traditions rigorously: no washing hanging out, any scandals hushed up by any and every means.

As the grandparents' sprawling bungalow in the old obsolete city, neglected and left to its dusty past, faded and crumbled, as they themselves did, some of its more superior assets made their way into the new dwelling to lend it some of the gravitas of the past: heavy, intricately carved pieces of furniture of rosewood and teak, carpets from Kashmir, silver filigree fingerbowls. Most certainly no altar, no god – unless safely BC. Artwork of an obligatory nature: lithographs in foxed browns and greys, framed in gilt, the work of English artists who had travelled through 'the mysterious East', of temples, palm trees, a stray elephant or camel. These must have been taken back to England to help retain memories of an ever receding time and place, then picked up in antique shops, and brought back – by whom, Grandfather or Father? – to represent History. Also the paintings called indiscriminately Moghul, Pahari, Rajasthani, of princes mounted on horses out on tiger hunts and princesses in gauzy dress pining on moonlit terraces for their return. They might have been museum pieces or they might have been painted for the tourist trade and sold on the pavements: no one knew or questioned their authenticity. Also, on polished tabletops, framed family photographs in which previous generations stared fishlike out of the inexorable wash of times past: women in saris with heavy brocade borders, their hair perfectly parted in the centre to make two drapes about their melancholy faces; men upright in tight suits, wearing expressions of power, possession and defiance: who would dare challenge them? Perhaps a child placed on a rug at their feet, reduced to a blur because it had given way to a yawn just as the shutter clicked.

None are known to you except two in a single small photograph in an oval silver frame placed on a square of tea-coloured crochet on Father's bureau next to his hairbrush: your grandparents, looking unrecognizably young, holding themselves stiffly in their wedding finery, displaying the stricken looks of newlyweds.

And now that you think of it, that pastel sketch of the woman on a bench in a park with a child playing at her feet, was the most recent, the only unimportant, valueless item amidst all the elaborately framed artwork, collected specifically to create an effect of success.

Here Mother, after the period of her absence – yes, that must be acknowledged – having reappeared (with a baby you were told was your sister Indu), stepped into Grand-mother's role and took on the duties of a 'company wife'. She too put the household 'on wheels' so that it ran as smoothly as Father's income and status required, although she showed no sign of Grandmother's pride in such an achievement, only of an unwilling martyrdom to his daily routine, that unbreakable routine of an executive's life: marching downstairs with a briefcase after a cup of coffee and two fried eggs on toast, to summon his designated driver out of the row waiting below who would take him to work and bring him back in the evening to what was supposedly the stability and order and monotony of the expected and the enforced.

Once he had left, Mother would call the cook to confer about the day's menu and make a shopping list to go with it. When he returned from the market with bags bulging with fruit and vegetables or leaking with the blood of fish, fowl or beast, she examined them all and took down the cost in a red notebook as was expected of her. The maid was given the washing to do and then carry up to the rooftop to dry. In the afternoon it was taken down to the ironing man who had set up his services in the shade of a neem tree in the street below. Later it was brought up in neatly folded armfuls smelling of starch and the heat of a coal-fired iron; payment was made item by item, all duly noted. Once a week larger items were collected by a washerman who took away sheets and towels and returned the following week, when the maid would change the bed linen. Any spots and tears would be pointed out and deductions made in his payment.

When Father returned from his work to this well-ordered home, he expected to be met by a wife prepared for the evening and the obligatory party (without which they would have been deemed social failures): either a party they threw or one they attended in one of the other executives' flats. The parties were identical; the party list varied only if one of their colleagues was transferred to another city or a new colleague appeared from one. The menu never varied: it was unthinkable to introduce any suspicious new item; any diminution of standards would be noticed and cause a disturbance, perhaps gossip.

When one of these events was held in your home,

you crouched on a stool in the kitchen and nibbled at the snacks the cook gave you on a plate, listening to the uproar in the dining and the drawing room of a party fuelled by food and drink – much food and more drink – voices rising higher and higher, laughter erupting or else arguments, equally alarming to you so that you crept off to bed, pulled the covers over your head and feared a riot had broken out from which you had better hide.

On the rare evenings when the family sat down to dinner by ourselves, Father sat at the head, visibly bored and depressed by the unimportance of the company. Once, you remember, Mother, after eyeing the mandatory meat and potatoes, rose and went to the kitchen, asked the cook if he would let her have some of the vegetables he had cooked for himself, and made a meal of it by herself under the threatening frown on Father's face. Words withheld.

Such incidents revealed her unsuitability as a wife. Father's family had established order; out of what disorder had she arrived?

She herself provided no clues, stubbornly silent when questioned. Something churlish about her, wasn't there? Where had she come from? Briefest mention was made of 'railway people', with no fixed address, constantly moved from one 'railway colony' to another, entered in one school for one term, in another the next, making friends only to lose them along the way. One had to have 'autograph books' to keep them, she allowed – with long, narrow pages, either pink or mauve or blue, on which friends and sometimes teachers inscribed a brief personal message or a poem of the 'roses are red, violets are blue' variety. Never an address. All of them known to be transient – like railway carriages. Once you met the daughter of such a family who spoke of the comforts, the luxury even, of the 'saloon cars' in which they travelled, accompanied by an entourage of attendants, but when you reported this to Mother, she shrugged, grimaced. Had *her* father been an engine driver, then? You and Indu made this suggestion when you were by yourselves and shouted with laughter that you quickly stifled.

But she must have seen, in whatever circumstances, much of the country, then? Surely she could talk of it to her daughters, desperate to break out of their own stationary situation, waiting for a whistle to blow, the lights to change so you could move on? 'I can't remember,' she claimed, abruptly ending all conjecture.

And what of family? Father had family, dominant, domineering. But what of hers? Pressed lips, guarded eyes, leading to a suggestion that there was something disreputable about it. What could it be? Had their skin colour been a shade too dark? That could have been quite enough of a reason for censure. If so, how could this marriage ever have taken place? If not arranged by the families in the accustomed way, then – a difficult premise – had they met and 'fallen in love'? As children of this marriage, you considered, then shied away from such an unlikely possibility, like ponies at the sight of a snake. In *those* days, you believed, parents did *not*. And could two less likely people have agreed to embark on such a hazardous adventure? Had no one warned them?

Now your eyes open to a possibility never considered before – that Father had once been young and able to consider romance and seen it in Mother being 'different', unlike what he was accustomed to, and been intrigued by that at some passing moment in his life, leading him to do something out of character, something rash.

It is the Stranger in the Jardín who has somehow re-awoken this question and perhaps unwittingly provided an answer: that Mother had been an art student, and brought a touch of adventure, some romance into the rigid routine of his life – till she went 'too far', even as far as Mexico, to study that art. If so, she had abandoned it – and now you recall that expression on her face that so seldom showed pleasure or became animated − of disappointment, distress, the look of failure, the failure that allowed Father to assume the look, the posture of success and, most importantly, the only success in that house.

This was how it was expected to continue, generation after generation, without change. This was what you had feared, and that fear falls upon you again like ashes, like sand that you had struggled to throw off and that compelled you to build your own individual life out of different elements − school, studies, exams, friends. Rushing out of the house with your books, returning to lock yourself into your room to study, prepare for the next exam, the next step. Then, when even those proved nothing but a variation of routine, order and monotony, seizing as if inspired on the study of languages that would wrench you out, lead you as far away as you could get − French that took you to Pondicherry, Portuguese that took you to Goa, and the Portuguese that led you to Spanish and Spanish had brought you here − *here* and *now*. *Aqui y ahora.*

So you swing your legs off the bed now, letting your feet find your slippers on the red-tiled floor, rise and push aside the bamboo curtain in the doorway onto the small veranda to catch the last of the day's incandescence lighting up the tumble of bougainvillea but withdrawing already to the bamboo grove beyond. The gardener has left with his broom and basket of sweepings. The maids have finished the day's labour and are leaving in a group, a gaggle, twittering with anticipation of the evening. Leaving, anticipating – as you too should, you must.

But instead you sink down on the *equipale* bench placed on the veranda and all you can see in that grove of dusk is Mother lying on a straw mat on the floor of a space off the bedroom called 'the boxroom'. If she is still there when Father emerges from the bedroom, fresh and ready for his morning cup of tea, he steps over her as if she is a rag left there carelessly, his face clenched tight as a fist. Has she been lying there all night? Only if you are up before anyone else do you see that figure supine on the mat, surrounded by boxes of various sizes, shapes and materials, all old, all battered. What had they contained? Her own artwork, sketches, pastels, remnants of it? And if so, what happened to them when the boxes were needed for a move? Had Cook summoned the kabariwallah off the street as he did periodically, to weigh bundles of scrap paper on his most dubious scales, and sold them for four rupees a kilo?

Mother, in that darkened flat, sitting up night after night after everyone else had gone to bed, a book open on her lap, her head propped up on one hand so no one can tell if she is reading or her eyes are shut. Then Father emerging from the bedroom, exasperation finally beyond control, to bark 'Headache again?' or 'Head falling off?' Did he grab the book from her and turn off the light? You were not there to see.

But now you beat your hands upon your knees and tell yourself: admit it, admit it! You heard, you saw through your half-open door, and you cried, 'Yes, yes. Hit her on the head with it! Beat her! Make her get up!'

Get up, get up, you tell yourself now, don't stop, keep moving. Return to your room and after a quick wash in the tiled bathroom, run a comb through your hair, snatch up your bag and leave the house that is now filling up with its residents returning from their walks, their tours, their shopping sprees, and dressing for dinner. You hear water running for baths, the hubbub in the kitchen area, the tables being set for dinner, the sounds of anticipation and preparation. Avoiding any encounter that might halt you, you let yourself out onto the street, hurry uphill towards a restaurant at the top where you will see people you don't know, hear voices and languages you can't decipher, and welcome the distractions of life.

It is a restaurant you have been to before. The waiter recognizes you and finds you a table in the corner suitable for dining alone, lights a candle on it with a flourish, brings you the menu and then the meal you order, as always with a tremor of fear and pride at your daring, at this learned accomplishment. The place, the occasion are all as friendly and unthreatening as you could wish, but you find yourself barely able to appreciate it. What it is is an obstruction, a postponement of what you really want to see, and hear, and attend to, so you cannot do any of it justice. The disappointed look on the waiter's face as he removes your plate with what you have left on it is a polite, silent rebuke.

Out on the street you find yourself still in a state of agitation. You hesitate, not wanting to return to your room; its emptiness will only oppress you, so you turn into the Jardín from where the daytime strollers and loiterers are mostly gone. No pigeons are strutting, no children running by with balloons, no popcorn vendors, even the ice-cream barrow at the corner idle, just a few lovers in the shadows, reluctant to leave, preoccupied with themselves.

It is as you want: lamplit, the Parroquia before you an

imperturbable silhouette against the evanescent stars, the trees still, silent.

Stay, sit, you tell yourself. Wait, here, now, she will appear and you will see her as she had never shown herself and you had never seen.

II

She looks through the mail lying on a tray by the front door. Sparse, quotidian. But one envelope stands out by its size, its clean crispness, an expensive elegance, addressed formally to both Mr and Mrs, so she has licence to indulge her curiosity and open it. The card it contains is gold-lined, handsome, and invites both to an event to be held at the Mexican embassy. How had it come to them? Perhaps Father had some commercial dealings – the world of trade a cat's cradle of improbable connections – and they would be of no interest to her. But the invitation is to a lecture organized by the cultural wing of the embassy, regarding a connection between the artists of the Mexican revolution and Indian artists of the freedom movement and Partition. One visiting Mexican art critic and one Indian art historian of repute are to address the subject.

She notes the day and time. Father pays it no attention. Besides, he will be out of town for a conference. She summons the driver and has him drive her up the calm, tree-lined avenues that run through the enclave of embassies and diplomats' residences designed by Sir Edwin Lutyens for what became the city of New Delhi. It is not a neighbourhood she often has cause to visit. Somehow she dares to proceed with the unusual venture and, having come so far, must now step out at the gate and let herself in by showing the invitation to a grave young man who waves her into a gathering of tastefully dressed and coiffed guests and hosts, the subdued murmur of civilized talk and laughter, trays passed around with iced drinks and little pieces of exquisite and unidentifiable food.

Knowing no one, she quickly takes a seat in the rows set up before a stage on the lawn, and is glad when the programme begins. There are the predictably pompous speeches made by career diplomats, a little guitar music and then the two critics come out to introduce the work of the artists – Mexican muralists who were inspired by and painted during the Revolution, and the Indian equivalent albeit of a later period – and then the flat, empty screen behind them that she had not earlier noticed comes silently, ominously to life.

The decorous tableau before it vanishes into a pit and what emerges is the artists' engagement with their history, in scene after scene of carnage: a knife-thrust here, a skull smashed open there, guts ripped from living bodies, drawing blood and more blood. Women's bodies are pierced and eviscerated, infants torn out of their wombs and arms, flung into flames, bones twisted and charred into ashes. Homes are levelled, wells destroyed, cattle left dead in ravaged fields. Out of these barbaric landscapes trains arriving, marvels of steel and technology, all smoke and fiery iron, some carrying troops and their arms, others packed with passengers slaughtered along the way, blood oozing out of carriages when they are opened, then more blood and still more. Victors climbing atop body-mountains, raising tattered flags, the flags that are required by nationhood. Mouths opening to roar: *Azadi! Libertad!* At their feet corpses left for vultures to gorge on. Wounds, mutilations thrust in the faces of those who survive to declare: this is Man, intrinsically, this is his history: look!

These slides leap, erupt into the polite scene, the discreetly lit dark. But it is not their incongruity that provides the shock for her. On the contrary, it is the confrontation with what she has always known and lived with. It is profoundly familiar, with masks and façades ripped away.

In the appalled silence that follows, before anyone can begin to move and speak, she has leapt to her feet and run, her hand crushed against her mouth to stop her from screaming. Out in the driveway, she stumbles, searching for her car and driver to take her away.

Anyone trying to explain might suggest that some wound that had been stitched up had split open then. Had the family witnessed that, it might have wondered if it had been accompanied by an admission of her own history, that suppressed one so carefully guarded. Why had it never been permitted to mention her family, its history? Perhaps she had, obliquely, timidly, and we, either innocently or maliciously, made up one of an endless train journey, with never a stop and no place of arrival.

Were those trains she saw on the screen with their unspeakable cargoes, the ones that could have carried the Muslims of India to Pakistan and the Hindus of Pakistan to India, also the ones that carried her family across some savage new border from which few arrived alive?

If so, she had refused to talk of it to anyone, ever. Not of a family, a home or a location. Had it been a desert, a mountain, an island? A mansion, a tenement? If there had been documents or photographs might they have been in those dusty, shabby cartons in the boxroom no one had thought of entering except her? Till Cook had emptied them and sold them to the kabariwallah for four rupees a kilo?

What had confronted her that night in the serene and stately garden was not the unknown and unimaginable but on the contrary what she had always known and always denied even to herself, but here saw fearlessly portrayed.

Fearlessness. That was what she now has to learn.

So she returns, again and again. Either because she cannot stay away or because her presence, her persistent interest has been noticed and invitations continue to arrive, circulars in the mail that she quickly intercepts and keeps to herself. She visits the library, withdraws books on art. It is noted by those who run the cultural division. Except for one, they are very young and charming and also enthusiastic. As part of their diplomatic agenda, they suggest she visit Mexico, so she may 'make a study of Mexican art, *casí no?*'. The invitation is casual, routine to them – scholarships are available – but to her it is a dare, a challenge. Having gone so far, she must go further. She accepts.

The challenge this creates to the home, the family – so solid, so unshakeable – is not one that is acknowledged or discussed. In another household it would have been, but this is one from which drama and melodrama have been banned, prohibited. An even grimmer, deeper silence descends, holds everyone in its grip as if by refusing to acknowledge what is happening. But as a volcano is subterranean till it is not, cracks appear. Rumours travel and come to the highest authority of all: Grandfather himself, seated at his massive desk, behind a barricade of files.

He is waiting with the fingertips of his two hands touching each other to form a turret. He does not look across at her, making clear her appearance is a distraction from what is important. But he has been briefed, he does not question. After a long silence encroached on only by the overhead fan's blades slowly ticking as regularly as a metronome, he parts his dry lips to speak. 'If that is your plan, then you must follow it,' he says in the voice of one who has always done exactly that.

Then, with an irritated movement, he drops his hands onto his files and opens the topmost one: there are many more he needs to go through. His secretary hurries to his side to take care of the one that is flung at him.

She is dismissed. Having received this wholly unexpected permission from the ultimate authority, she can do nothing other than to pursue what he had termed her 'plan', even if she was barely aware of having made one.

Having received permission from one who could not be denied, she soon finds herself clutching her passport, her visa, her ticket, a bag, her fear and her nerve, doing what till the very last she had not believed she could do, stepping into the sinister metal capsule that stands waiting on the tarmac to swallow her, finds her seat, straps herself into it – the motherly flight attendant helping one so obviously a novice – and finds it lifting off terra firma into the dust-shrouded Delhi night and sets off to explore the vast invisible vacuum.

What follows seems to take place in one long confusing blur leading to her arrival in the night at a door set in a high stone wall where a watchman is waiting to light her way in, past a harshly lit room with an unoccupied reception desk, down a dimly lit veranda encroached on by invading plants as in a jungle, to a room where she falls onto a narrow bed to be engulfed at last by exhaustion, sleep and sorrow as if into her natural element, certain she would never wake from it.

Then woken, after all, by daylight, the murmur of a dove in the tangle of foliage at the window, the sound of water falling somewhere and a broom brushing on tiles.

She can recognize nothing – this narrow wooden bed spread with thick white cotton sheets on which she has slept, and now woken, alone.

Her relief so keen she almost moans aloud as at a thrust at her ribs of revelation. Every moment of her life so far has been removed, wiped out, allowing this moment. The rest of her life will be a pursuit of the recovery of it.

But now you are allowing your own experience of that journey to substitute hers. You have not yet recovered her experience of it.

III

It is time to search out the Stranger. How and why did you rebuff her when she offered friendship? How could you have turned your back on her, an old woman, disbelieving her? You have learnt now that you would like to believe her, yes.

It is not difficult to find her. She is of course in the first place that you look: in the Jardín, on a bench where she is basking catlike in the sun like all the others who live under the spell cast by the rose-pink Parroquia and its eccentric bells. She beckons to you gaily when she sees you appear. 'Darling, I've been waiting—' she growls, patting a seat beside her. 'What have you been doing – painting?' she guesses coquettishly.

You perch beside her and remind her that you are here as a language student, not an art student.

'Not like *mamacita*, then?' she sighs, narrowing her yellow eyes and thinning her dark-brown lips, indicating how disappointed your mother would have been with your choice. You assure her once again that she had never been a painter.

'Ah, but *here* she was,' she cries with conviction. '*Here* she was an *artista*! I first saw her here, here, standing before her easel, painting this scene, the Jardín, the children playing—'

'Where was she staying then? I want to see. Show me,' you urge her, determined to test her veracity.

She becomes nervous then, fiddling with her enormous necklace and its even more enormous pendant, and the chunks of coral and turquoise on her fingers, creating a rattle to distract you from your stubborn insistence.

'Let us have lunch together, then go there,' you persist.

But lunch barely interests her now. After pushing around forkfuls of pasta and making disgusted faces at it, she leaves most of it uneaten, preferring to pull out a cigarillo and beckon the waiter to light it for her, then moodily withdraws behind its curls of smoke. But you will not give up, you wait till, with a sigh, she gets up and collects her hat and satchel while you pay.

She appears to wilt, turning into a shadow, losing all

colour, all animation. She walks slowly, unwillingly, as if each step on the cobbled street hurts her feet, and quite probably it does. She mutters to herself words you cannot quite make out.

You are all the way down at Parque Juárez and you think she might be planning to enter it and take a rest under the trees, but no, at the gate she veers off along another cobbled street, a narrow one where houses crowd together and there are sounds of maids sweeping, canary birds twittering, water trickling down from rooftop gardens. But you do not stop at any of their doors to knock; instead she pauses at a heavily locked gate and both of you stand and peer through its bars. It looks onto a vacant lot. A house might well once have stood there but now it is a scene of absence – a plot of scrubby soil where the remains of a house and the lives lived in it can barely be deciphered: a single piece of wall left standing, tiled as in a bathroom, a few paving stones with weeds growing in the cracks, one yellowing tree. A pair of motherless kittens seated on what had been a step, wide-eyed with hunger and waiting.

The Stranger can barely move her trembling lips to speak. She points through the bars and whispers, 'It *was* there once.'

'But there's nothing here now. What happened?'

'It belonged to the family Garcia. It was once a grand house – carved doors, many courtyards, balconies, gardens. They used to take in foreign students. Who knows, some might have been troublemakers. I did hear the family sold it but I do not know where they went. Why must everything end like this?' she breaks into a wail. 'Everyone I knew, gone. New people, new houses, hotels, shops. I am a stranger here. This is San Miguel now. Ah, ah, oh, oh-h,' she groans theatrically, her hand to her throat. Had she been an actress once? you wonder, not for the first time. Was this a scene she was acting in her own play? But really, if her disappointment is not genuine, yours is.

You had resisted her fantastical tale but now find you would like to believe it. Could she, like a wizard or a magician, bring your mother to life again even if it is a life you never knew or suspected?

You can't let her off now. You take her to the park for a rest and continue to question her. Where was the school where she studied under the Maestro?

'Sometimes a studio in Bellas Artes, sometimes one in the Instituto Allende. Here, there' – she stammers – 'and then she left. With some other students.'

'Left? Went where?'

'They said, to make another school, another kind of school—'

'And did they? Where was it? Can we go and see it?'

'Oh no, no, no,' she cries in alarm – necklace, bracelets, pendant all clanking, 'it is too, too far. Outside town. Difficult to reach.'

'How far? Can't we take a bus, a taxi?' You are on fire to see it, to uncover the truth – or the falsehood – of what she has been telling you. 'Why not? Why not? I *want* to.'

She rises from the bench quickly and straightens her many skirts and scarves in agitation. 'I am tired, my *chica*. It is time to go home, rest now.'

'Yes, yes, but another day? Tomorrow? No? Next week, then?'

You will, you must follow the trail. If it has all been a cruel joke, you will not let her evade it. You take a sharper tone and arrange to meet next at the bus stop outside the Iglesia de San Francisco.

Waiting there in the shade of laurel trees, you find yourself tense with anxiety and anticipation, even sweating a little in the dry desert air of the altiplano. Will a bus appear? Will *she* appear? There are others who are waiting quite patiently, carrying market bags filled with their shopping, passing the time by buying packets of *chicle* and paper cones filled with peanuts. A young woman, elegantly dressed and coiffed, circles them with a tray filled with coloured jellies in little glasses and tries to sell you one. Children are chasing pigeons around the fountain, arousing furious flutters and offended mutters. No one seems anxious or impatient. Everyone takes it as an interlude to be enjoyed.

This increases your tension but, as invariably happens, when you decide to give up in exasperation and walk away, she does appear, although it takes you a moment or two to recognize her: she is dressed all in black and brown and has somehow retreated behind the dark covering as if she planned to travel incognito. The face that looks out from the rebozo she has wrapped about her head is lined with age and pain. If it is a camouflage then she has entirely assumed one of a Mexican *anciano*.

But you remain firm: you will not let her retreat. When the bus arrives and collapses to a halt, you grasp her by her arm and help her up the step behind the women with their market bags, the mothers with their sweetly asleep babies, the wide-eyed children and the shuffling old men, and find seats for yourselves. She shrinks back into herself, silent, and you stare out of the window feeling both triumphant and mean.

The town gradually dwindles till its small concrete houses painted pink and purple and green, strung along the dusty road behind their gates of iron scrollwork or low walls of volcanic rock or high hedges of cacti, are left behind and there are only the ubiquitous motor workshops and warehouses, the occasional *rosticería*, *tiendas* selling tortillas and bottled drinks and open stalls displaying mounds of fruit cut open to entice thirsty travellers in the buses that stop. Eventually these peter out and you are in the open campo lying flattened under the equally flattened and open sky. You are pressed between them and yet the highway somehow cuts through, a persistent worm. On either side some fields have been ploughed but others are bare, blackened by the fires that burnt the stubble. Rows of poplar trees run along canals that are invisible, obscured as they are by dusty reeds from which an occasional heron takes off, trailing its long mosquito legs. Here and there, willows droop around a well. Some small ranchos with burros standing behind fences, heads lowered in sleep or dejection.

The highway and the land it traverses seem infinite but on the distant horizon hills appear like the incoming waves of a prehistoric sea, changing in colour from grey to blue and back to grey, their folds closed about their secrets, the histories they do not display. Only a small white church with a cupola and a bell tower on one hill, simply a cross on another. Will you travel up to them, through and beyond them, and come upon the revelation you seek?

You begin to grow uneasy at the distance you have covered. Who could have considered setting up an art school here? But just as you are about to sink into glum frustration, someone standing on the roadside flags down the bus. It halts and lets in a young woman wearing a beret that she takes off and walks down the aisle with, singing a ballad that stirs everyone into wakefulness. They murmur to each other, extract coins from the depths of their clothing and drop them into the beret she holds out to them, or encourage their children to do so. She pours these into the receptacle for fares, the bus slows to a halt, she jumps off and disappears down an invisible path. How can this not encourage you, even if all the land has to show now is cacti – cacti twisted, cacti in lumps, cacti so grey and stark they seem carved out of the stones and rubble lying around? The young balladeer had brought life, energy, promise with her: it exists!

Aroused, you sit up, persuade yourself of a reality that had been dwindling and fading hour by hour, mile by mile. You had almost allowed it to vanish. But now you feel determined to pursue it, capture and verify it. It mattered. Turning to your companion, you urge her to tell you if she is sure we are on the road we were meant to take. She herself seems uncertain, mumbles, 'I came here once but that was long ago . . .'

Just then the bus does make a stop, at a signpost that says, improbably, *Los Encuentros*, and the driver calls back over his shoulder to confirm this is the stop you require. So you dismount, stiff and shaky, the only passengers to do so, and it is with some relief and some trepidation that you make out a barbed-wire fence with a gate in it that is hanging open.

You enter it and find a small chapel, or what must once have been a chapel although it is now a ruin. The stucco walls had once been painted white, the door and windows edged with red, all faded now, the walls covered with graffiti, the windowpanes broken. The two of you stand in the dust and stare at the cacti-strewn landscape, then make out the shambles of a row of adobe huts, corrugated-iron roofs sliding off them. In the distance a building that is somewhat larger and has a long veranda with a roof that had once been tiled. The doors along it are gaping open; you can see that the rooms are empty except for fallen tiles and timbers, all deep in dust. There are steps leading up to it but you hesitate to move towards it.

Your companion, however, raises her head with a horse-like motion and begins to hobble towards it up a path edged with bricks, so you follow.

'This is, this *was* the art school?'

Both of you sink down on a step and she lowers her head into her shoulders and sends out whimpering and undecipherable laments from there. To revive her you open up your bag and take out the bottles of water, the juice boxes and packets of biscuits you have prudently brought to share with her. She looks up at the sight of them and even appears grateful.

A little goat that has been unobtrusively nibbling at the fringes of this scene gives a sudden start and, with its hooves skittering on the stones and rubble, quickly disappears.

Your companion is drinking juice and eating biscuits with a shaking hand and you try to keep your voice neutral when you begin the necessary interrogation.

'*This* was the new art school? And Mother came *here*? With whom? Who were the other students?'

Her head immediately begins to shake so violently you cannot help suspecting her of theatrics. But by prodding you do manage to extract a few details, not necessarily reliable, of course: of the house where she lodged to which some men came out of nowhere, strangers with long hair, sandals. 'Jee-ayes' they were called. Did I know that word – 'jee-ayes, jee-ayes?' They said they had come to paint like many other gringos did, but they did not look like them. And they talked – always – of war. 'Where?' you ask. 'Who knows where? Far, far, not here. Here we had Rev-o-lu-tion, not war. They did not come to paint our beautiful town, they wanted to paint this war, vi-o-lence. Once they had a show, so bad, so ugly. And they per-su-aded your little *mamacita*, my pretty Rosita, to leave San Miguel for an artists' commune they said they would build and where they would paint these terrible pictures. Not our flowers, our fountains, like other artists made but *ruinas*, bones, stones!' – throwing out her hands with some of her old vigour. 'Guns, bombs and killing, killing!'

'And trains? Did they paint trains?'

Who spoke? Where did those words come from? You have fallen silent but the Stranger heard them, looks puzzled. 'Trains? Trains did take part in our Rev-o-lu-tion but they knew nothing about that. They painted planes, planes dropping bombs, burning homes, killing people. When I came to find her and saw all this they were doing here' – again throwing out her hands to condemn the scene – 'I

47

asked her why, why? And she told me it is not right to only paint flowers, fountains. I asked why, what is wrong with them? And she began to cry, *la pobrecita*, and talk of terrible things, of refugees, killing and vio-lence . . .' She stops to wipe the sweat pouring down her forehead and into her eyes and down to her mouth.

'Where? Where?' you ask. 'In India? At Partition – did she tell you?' but, as you feared, she has no answer.

All she does add is 'And she had grown so thin, all bones, and burnt black. No shoes, barefoot like a beggar. *This* I could *not* allow! I told her I will take you away at once, to San Miguel. If I leave you here you will fall ill.'

After a while, letting her collect her composure – and you yours – you ask as quietly as you can, 'And she came back with you? To San Miguel?'

Instead of answering, she gets to her feet and begins to beat the dust out of her skirts and stamp it out of her boots as if she is beating the bad *hombres* out of a nightmare. 'We must go!' she orders so fiercely that a grackle on the roof takes off with a squawk and a lizard leaps up from a stone onto another. 'We cannot miss the bus!'

She begins to hobble quite speedily and you find your-self running after her, infected by her frenzied haste and fear, to the bus stop. It arrives, you heave her up the step ahead of you, look for vacant places and this time take the window seat. When you have managed to open it to let in some air, even if along with sand and dust and grit, and begun to breathe more evenly, you decide to ask her one more question. Turning to her as she sits resuming the pose of the *anciano*, you ask, to let her know you are not satisfied, 'And the Maestro? She returned to his school?'

'The Maestro?' she sighs, as if in sorrow, but you suspect she has no answer and is giving herself time to invent one. 'Ah, aah. A new student had come. From Hungaria, she said. Blonde, long blonde hair, so blonde. She said she had come to study painting with the Maestro. People say she told him she was a contessa, very rich, and she would open a studio for him – in Hungaria! And one day –' with a loud clap of her hands, she ends – 'and one day they were both of them – gone!'

Enough now. It is time to say: Enough!

You sink back in your seat and shut your eyes to the flying dust. This woman, this stranger, she is after all nothing else but a Trickster. A very, very canny one. She has taken up enough of your time and your gullibility and now you must turn your back on her – firmly. You do not need more of her fantasies and falsehoods, they have caused you pain. She does not know how much.

When she places a hand on your knee, you think that without its usual carapace of rings and bracelets, it resembles nothing so much as a scorpion, a dead, dry scorpion with its sting intact. You shake it off.

You had different reasons to come here – before you were misled. You have other occupations: your Spanish classes. Placing your notebook, your pencils, your dictionary in your sling bag, you set off for the language school down the hill in the dazzle of morning light reflected in the water splashed across the pink paving stones by industrious maids up and down the streets and still smelling freshly of soapsuds. Other students are making their way to it too, from their separate lodgings. The schoolroom is different from the ones in the universities where you have studied: the students, who sit in a semicircle around the teacher, are made up of elderly retired tourists and visitors, some American and many Canadian, those with a more serious bent than the ones happy to while away their time on benches in the Jardín and the cafés in the arcades. And what a pleasure it is to be led through your exercises by a teacher so young and so lively, who breaks up the monotony of verbs and tenses by teaching you such cheerful exclamations as '*hay chocola!*' and '*hay chihuahua!*' to go with vigorous smacks of the hands.

After the morning class the students break into groups and wander off to lunch. You find yourself drawn to the company of the single other young woman in the class and the only one not from Canada or the US but from the Philippines. Her name is Isabel and she is here to make a comparative study, she tells you, of the Spanish spoken in her country and that of Mexico, both with their colonial past, she explains. Together you wander down to the mercado de San Juan de Dios for a burrito or a bowl of *guisado*.

But, through the shimmer of steam rising from the row of great cooking pots, you glimpse a face peering at you with a knowing, cunning smile, and are jolted into spilling a spoonful of scalding gravy on yourself. Turning away with Isabel who beckons you to survey the display of magic potions, herbs and soaps on the neighbouring stall, you find something disquietingly familiar about the whiskered *anciano* who points out which one will bring you true love, which one wealth, the death of a rival or whatever else you may need, and for all its enticements insist on moving on urgently.

It becomes unexpectedly hazardous to set out on what are meant to be pleasant explorations of a town so foreign

ANITA DESAI

to you that it promised to be free of any ties to your past
and your origins. Even browsing in the aisles of the *biblio-
teca* you feel someone's breath upon your neck as soft and
stealthy as a cat's paw, someone discreetly peering to see
what books you have chosen.

Everywhere you go, you glimpse out of the corner
of your eye that unmistakable figure emerging from the
stones and the shadows into the dazzling light of day like
a mirage created by it but also easily dispelled by it. She
assumes the persona of the woman circling the Jardín,
tirelessly proffering an armload of necklaces, pleading with
you to buy. As well as the woman sunk down on the door-
step of a bank, a basket to receive alms at her knobby feet
in their broken sandals.

It makes you trip but Isabel walks by, her eyes drawn
to the allure of the further scene. On the day of your last
class that you mark by lunching after it in the Italian restaurant on the patio of a venerable old hotel, amongst
potted orange and lemon trees and cages of aged macaws,
and after promising to stay in touch, you wander together
through the extensive grounds of what had once been the
garden house of an old and wealthy family whose crest in
stained glass hangs above the arched doorway, and come
upon a long corridor that runs along the boundary wall

with doors opening into rooms that appear uninhabited. But at the far end of it you are brought to a sudden halt by coming upon that ominous figure now in the guise of a ghost bending to feed a swarm of cats that flock around her feet hungrily, all the while clucking in a motherly manner unknown to you: can *that* be her too?

You clutch Isabel's plump arm in its lace sleeve, stopping her from going further. She is given to smiling and chatting with everyone she meets and you know she loves cats too, and she looks at you in query. You hiss, 'Stop. I don't want to meet her.' Isabel looks puzzled and asks, 'Who?' as if she sees no one, but lets you make an abrupt turn, expecting her to follow you through the arched doorway where she asks, 'Why?' That is the question you ask yourself, but instead ask Isabel, 'Is this still a hotel? Do people stay in those rooms?'

'It seems,' she replies, 'a few do. I think mostly old people who have lived here for years and are going nowhere.' Of the many lives you made up for the Stranger, that of 'an old person going nowhere' was not one you had considered. Yet she had seemed to belong there utterly.

With the Spanish classes over and Isabel gone and the advanced class not yet begun, you have little to do but explore the town as a tourist, going into shops to look at postcards, jewellery, scarves, baskets of carved wooden spoons, engraved glass, masks of straw and carved in wood with fierce aspects . . . Such excursions are tiring, you find, and you make frequent stops at the ice-cream barrows that offer flavours you had not known existed – chilli, tequila, *tamarindo, elote* – but refreshing as they are, the refreshment evaporates quickly, leaving you unsatisfied, wishing for more, something else. You want, you want, but *what* do you want?

After a while you restrict your walks to the Parque Juárez, sometimes early in the morning when it is still so fresh the day seems not to have wholly emerged from its sleep but still to be dreaming. The paths wind in and out of stands of palm trees and drooping Peruvian pepper trees, lined with beds of lilies and oleanders. Once you encounter an androgynous figure dressed in black tights and a blouse with the billowing sleeves of a bullfighter, absorbed in slowly waving a crimson cape and advancing with a sword towards the effigy of a bull carved in wood. Another time, a slim figure in white pyjamas performing the trance-like motions of t'ai chi that make it appear flight is no illusion.

If you go in the late afternoon the paths are overtaken

by industrious dog walkers and exercise devotees, often groups of women keeping up a brisk pace in their gym shoes while chattering just as briskly. You avoid the playground where music is blaring at top volume to encourage toddlers on swings and jungle gyms to scream much louder than they are accustomed to doing, and walk past the benches occupied by assiduous lovers – young, middle-aged and elderly too, all equally in the throes of *amor*, to where there is a quietly trickling fountain and you may expect to find only the sedate, secretively gossiping doves in the gathering dusk.

There you sink down on a bench, so deep in thoughts that come from a great distance away that you only gradually become aware of someone beside you, as if your thoughts had conjured her into being, half obscured as she is by a vast straw hat and voluminous skirts of lace and cotton and tulle, umber, cinnamon, saffron and indigo. Slowly a face turns to you with a great beam of yellowing teeth.

'*Querida!*' she purrs, 'there you are! I have been waiting,' and before you can construct a resistance, you find your neck encircled by her arms, her hand weighted with massive silver rings planted on your knee, her eyes ablaze so you think you might be turned to a flake of ash by her gaze. 'Bonita, *chica*,' she says huskily, 'I have something to tell you – you will be *so* excited!'

And immediately you suspect that the excitement will be bad for you, dangerous, but she does not release you and somehow, instead of struggling, you almost willingly, weakly agree to her continuing. '*Chica*, I have made a plan to take you to see my home in Colima! The house I grew up in, where I took your mama too. Very, very different from where I live now,' she adds coyly (*had* she seen you that day you wandered through the grounds of the old hotel and came upon her feeding the tribe of cats and then quickly turned away and disappeared? Nothing could be beyond her, her stagecraft, her omniscience). 'My *sobrino* lives in it now and when I told him who was visiting me here in San Miguel' – she tickles your chin playfully – 'he said I must bring you to Colima. We will go, my Bonita, we *must*! It will be a *wonderful* excursion – not like the sad one we took to *Los Encuentros*. We should not have gone *there*.' She pats your knee reassuringly. 'That is why I want to take you in another direction en-tire-ly, and from there you can continue to La Manzanilla—'

'La Manzanilla?'

'But yes, my darling, that is where your mother went too, after stopping in Colima, to recover from the illness she contracted on that rancho where she was living with *los locos*, to paint again as she had learnt from the Maestro. By the sea! So brave, so mar-vell-ous! After that,' she admits, lowering her voice, 'I did not see her again. But she sent you to me, my *chica*, so now I will take you too to my family home in Colima and it will be – how do you say – *fun!*'

You make a floundering attempt to resist, to refuse, but also you feel yourself weakening, going limp. What excuses can you make? Your classes are over, you have no reason to stay on here, you must move on. And you hear yourself asking for details of such a journey and rouse yourself to insist that this time you will travel comfortably. You will go yourself to Viajes Mexico, the travel agency, and make the arrangements. And of course pay for them. After having had that glimpse of how she lived, how could you not? Also, you need to have some control, you cannot surrender it all to her, even if you let her lead the way.

When you finally get up and get away, a little shakily, you wonder if this is what Mother would have wanted you to do in your pursuit of her – and then realize how far you have been dragged into a fantasy of her life. But is it her fantasy, or yours? Yours or the Trickster's?

You do not sleep that night.

IV

The Trickster insists you take the window seat of the little plane so you can look out onto a lunar landscape of volcano upon volcano emerging as they must have done in that prehistoric age of creation and then see it enter the stage of mountain ranges, forests, plunging cliffs and deep arroyos – the world in the making beneath you in your airborne carriage.

You cannot stop yourself from crying out in amazement upon seeing rise out of it the snow-clad cone of the Volcan de Fuego that now floats in the air, miraculously untethered to the canyons and forests below.

The Trickster sits back, smiling, drinking from a bottle of orange soda and looking as pleased as if she had created it all for your pleasure. It has even eclipsed the shock you had when you went to collect her in a taxi to the airport, unrecognizable without her tiered skirts, her scarves, her bandanas and ornaments, dressed instead in a black dress with gilt buttons, almost militaristic, a bit rusty with age but clearly once fashionable, and even stockings and buckled shoes. Now what role was she setting out to play, you had asked yourself and she had smiled and smiled and wouldn't say.

And now the plane is coming down to land on the flat grey-green Pacific coastline, so close to the ocean you think the plane might run into it for a spectacular finale, and that would be as great a joy as flying, as you have done, flying like an eagle, a Mexican eagle over and around the volcano. When you step down the ladder onto the tarmac, the light on the ocean comes up in a great wave to strike you with its fierce, aggressive heat and the air thrums with it and makes you unsteady. You find yourself laughing as you run with your fellow travellers into the shade of the little terminal building. There has never been an arrival of such dazzling promise. *Bienvenido, bienvenido* indeed!

A taxi takes you on the next stage of your journey along a highway lined with coconut groves and banana plantations with the heavy noonday light glittering upon them like torrential rain, small clusters of tin- and straw-roofed huts, cattle drowsily grazing in a field speckled with white egrets, then whitewashed walls painted with garish murals and advertisements for Coca-Cola, a veterinary clinic, a school, of course a church and another church, towers and cupolas painted white, walls blue and pink and yellow.

The road has been climbing gradually and the houses you pass have been growing larger, more elaborate; the traffic has increased: it is clear you have arrived. Ringed by stately government office buildings with deep arcades and an hotel as white and elaborate as if fashioned out of coral, its balconies trimmed with iron scrollwork, below it the plaza, so much larger and grander than the one in the town you have left; it makes you realize you are now in the state capital, not a little provincial one. Set in the middle of lawns ringed by palm trees is a bandstand like a painted birdcage on a pedestal, its birds all flown. There are not many people around at this hour; they will more likely emerge later for the *dansant* and the music.

'Yes,' the Trickster confirms excitedly. 'See, see, that is where we would dance – when I was young. I brought my Rosarita here too; everyone would stare, she was so pretty when she danced the tango with the young men—' and with those words she manages to wreck the whole picture: Mother dancing the tango on a lamplit Mexican night, a man's leg thrust between hers – she asks you to believe *that*?

You grimace as ferociously as you know how to let her see what you think of her absurdities. You have also had the first intimation that she is not done with her tricks; you must be on the alert and prepared.

The taxi has driven past the plaza and now stops at a massive carved door studded with medieval locks and bolts: it is the house she has claimed is her birthplace. But when you turn to her to make the next move, you find her smile too has grown strained; she is clenching her teeth over her lower lip and her trembling fingers give away her nervousness when she reaches up to ring the doorbell. You grow tense too, wondering whether to expect a repeat of the experience of visiting the artists' rancho – or what she had claimed had been one.

But this time you are not disappointed. On the contrary, just as she had promised, you are awed when the door is opened by a smiling young woman in a pretty shift dress who greets her fondly and you see beyond the hall, which is shadowy after all the sunlight you have come through, to a paved courtyard, orange and lemon trees in great clay pots placed around a fountain blue and yellow with painted Talavera tiles, and wrought-iron tables and chairs set in the shade of pomegranate trees.

This was your home? you nearly gasp, stopping yourself because it would not be polite to seem so incredulous. The Trickster however is restored by the sight and smiles with pride.

A slim dark man with patrician silver streaks in the hair at his temples and an exquisitely trimmed moustache comes out of a room near the entrance on silent shoes to welcome you and greet his aunt with both reticence and punctiliousness. The Trickster, no such reticence about her, throws her arms out to embrace him. You see him produce a tight semblance of a smile, accepting her embrace with well-bred politeness – not effusive but dutiful – while she responds with enthusiasm enough for both, loudly smacking her lips even if he does not offer his cheek to accept them.

A grackle, perched on a fig tree, lets out a sharp, sarcastic whistle to express its opinion of the scene.

Aunt and nephew exchange greetings in Spanish, then take note of you standing to the side, awkward, and break into English.

'My young friend, Arturo, I told you I would bring her – Rosarita's daughter, can you believe she has come?

All the way from India! I found her in the Jardín in San Miguel, just as if Rosarita had sent her to me – here she is, here she is!' She insists on drawing you into what is, despite her effort, not quite a circle. You put out your hand to shake his, he bends slightly as if he were about to kiss it and you wonder if there is not a slight suggestion of irony in his attitude, his small smile, his lifted eyebrows, and a hint of doubt as well, but you see he is a man incapable of impoliteness. Is he an actor too, like his aunt? You remind yourself – again – to be on your guard.

'Both the rooms in my hotel – my palazzo' – again that hint of irony – 'are free. The señora and señorita may choose whichever they please,' he declares and calls upon Marisol the maid to carry their bags – looking so inferior and dusty – across the courtyard to the rooms that are on a raised terrace at the far end of it, handing her giant keys from another century to open them.

The Trickster is beside herself with excitement. She has no scarves and ornaments to fling about with joy but her eyes are ablaze as a wolf's might be if reflecting firelight. 'Ah, ah, the room my *tío* and *tía* had – I will sleep in it tonight! Will that suit you, my darling? Will you like the other one? But you must see both first, of course you must!'

The two rooms face each other across the terrace. You stand by as Marisol opens one and then the other with her medieval iron keys that clank dramatically, and the great carved doors swing open to reveal their interiors. These make you and even the Trickster fall silent with awe: everything about them is on a scale that makes you aware of your own minor, negligible size, your inappropriateness, marks of a lesser race. Each room has, in its centre, a four-poster bed the size of a seaworthy barque, the mahogany posts carved into a wilderness of vines. Mosquito nets – you have seen none since you left India – are draped over them to remind you that you are now in the tropics. In the corners of each room are armoires with long mirrored panels, and carved dressers and chests large enough to hold the most impressive dowries. Beyond these rooms are bathrooms nearly half their size, with mosaic flooring, basins and tubs of Talavera tiles and fittings of brass in the forms of fish, frogs and mermaids. The shuttered doors open onto a stretch of lawn below the terrace, walled, and over the wall you see rooftops falling down a slope into groves and fields and the hills beyond.

The Trickster, who has been standing on the threshold of one, gazing at the scene, turns to you. 'This, this is the room where my *tío* and *tía* slept,' she whispers. You almost expect her to genuflect.

'Of course you must have it,' you assure her, and have the maid carry your bags to the room across from it, and really it will do just as well; there is no difference between the two, both expressive of colonial history and its splendour.

You will have your baths, then meet Arturo in the inner courtyard; he has offered you dinner, although it occurs to you that this casa on the edge of town, without any visible guests, hardly appears to function like a hotel. It is still rather like a family home but one with the family gone, the house remaining – a mausoleum.

After a long bath in a luxurious amount of water, gushing out of the taps and spilling over you in such plenitude as though it is a gift to you, then dressing in the best clothes you have with you – and you are quite aware they are not adequate to the scene (shoes? no shoes? just sandals? better to go barefoot!) – you go out to the edge of the terrace at the back and look across to where the shadows of the columnar cypress trees are beginning to lengthen, as the sun is lowering itself towards the horizon to merge with the blue twilight of the hills beyond. Flocks of parrots are settling in the fruit trees with a cacophony of shrieks to announce their arrival and their claim to their territory.

You stay very still and breathe deeply and slowly, trying to see if Mother's presence here once has left any trace of itself. But as the sun sinks into the sunless hours, you cannot dispel the doubts that have followed you every step of the journey. How could she have come on this adventure without uttering a word to you, to any of her family, then return simply to resume the life she knew? How could it be possible to live parallel lives with no apparent connection? How could she not have left any clue other than the Trickster's tales, which have led you nowhere? Dare you ask her nephew if he had ever been host to her? Now *that* would provide the corroboration you need. Here she comes, blown along on a cloud of heavy, heady perfume, draped once again in her familiar swirl of pink and green and violet skirts, now topped by a velvet *huipil* lavishly embroidered all over with flamboyant roses and hibiscus blooms, peacock-feather earrings swinging down to her shoulders. Her mouth is painted a crimson that is almost black, her eyes outlined theatrically with kohl. A construction, you see, put together to dazzle or else to show herself equal to her ancestral home.

And she bends over to kiss you, uttering cries as shrill

as those of the parrots who simultaneously fall silent as if the curtain has descended on them, allowing her to assume her place centre stage. 'Come, come, my darling, the table has been set for us,' she rouses you, truly as if this is all a piece of theatre she has arranged. But for whom? You hardly feel worthy.

In the inner courtyard you find a table set with linen, silver and china, all of which look as if they were family heirlooms. Candles have been lit in glass sconces, gardenias arranged for a centrepiece. When Arturo appears – quickly, unobtrusively – and asks you to be seated, it turns out that just as unobtrusively an elegant dinner has been prepared – ceviche in small glass goblets, turkey in a *mole* speckled with sesame seeds, a crisp salad of jicama, little dishes of mandarin oranges in wine to follow. The young woman who helped to seat you and spread a linen napkin across your lap is now introduced as Caroline, his daughter who is training for a career in hotel management – 'all so new to us', he modestly admits. She withdraws politely, possibly a little bored, leaving the Trickster to dominate.

Perhaps you drink a little too much of the excellent wine with which your host has been filling and refilling your glass. Perhaps you have not really been following the conversation, intent as you are on the enjoyment of so refined a meal – after all the years of making do with whatever there was – but the question you have been determined to ask tonight if you are ever going to leave it to rest, slips out of your reach.

You find you have not really been taking in the tenor or the trajectory of the dialogue between your two fellow diners. For a while they are punctilious about making it at least slightly intelligible to their guest – questions about the fate and fortunes of others in the family, it seems – but when they realize these are not comprehensible to you, slipping into Spanish. So although you have ceased to try to decipher any of it you do become aware of a change in the conversation as one might become aware of the hard seat or back of one's chair, making you increasingly uncomfortable and prodding you to pay attention and see if you can make a discreet escape.

Arturo, from being quietly if somewhat ironically respectful towards his aunt, has become tense, terse, no longer the dutiful nephew but instead the representative of a distinctly different aspect of the Trickster's past. And she, from being effusive, has become aggressive, accusatory. '*Mi madre, mi padre,*' she is insisting, clasping her hands to her velvet- and rose-covered bosom, throwing the words like knives across the table at him, 'they *knew*, they *said*, you cannot make a hotel out of two rooms! Is it prac-tic-al? Is it the way to make it pro-fit-able?'

He has moved the salt cellars placed in front of him from an inch to the left to an inch to the right with his immaculately manicured fingers. 'You have a proposal, aunt?'

'No, no, no, not I! But you will remember, my dear *sobrino*, when *mi padres* were alive, *they* had plans, *they* wanted to make a hotel *grande* – a rival to the hotel on the plaza, and that would be good for us *all*, would it not? Then we could *all* be rich, not just one but *all*!'

So those are the positions they have taken up, in separate camps, prepared for combat. It makes the nephew more erect and tense and very, very still. A mistake: it makes the Trickster more shrill, more voluble, gesturing with abandon. A new suspicion assails you: is *this* the reason the Trickster had manipulated you into accompanying her to Colima – to be witness to a matter of inheritance, family rivalry and injustice? Every combatant needs support.

You grow increasingly uneasy, wanting to leave, to seize something of the evening to yourself. How are you to do that? One seems to need you to see how she has been cheated out of her legacy, the other to dismiss you, politely, as an irrelevance. You become desperate to rise to your feet, put away your napkin and ask to be excused, when the nephew himself decides to bring the unseemly scene to a close and suggests it is time for the guests to retire, they are surely tired and did they not say they had ordered a taxi to take them to La Manzanilla early next morning?

So you feel excused from the scene of a melodrama but when you rise to leave, you hear a chair fall – a wrought-iron chair that falls with a great clang – and turn to see the Trickster on her back on the paving stones, her skirts and petticoats up, flailing and wailing. You have to rush back to pull down her garments so the nephew may put her back on her feet. Now she collapses against him and weeps, begs, pleads – but you can't follow her speech, so distorted by sobs and tears. He grasps her by one arm, you by the other and together you bring her across the courtyard and up the terrace to her room. He opens the door and turns to you to see to her but she is too destroyed to be helped to wash or change and all you can do is lead her to her bed, hoist her onto it with all your own strength, remove her shoes, pull up her covers and leave her to her disgrace.

As you turn to leave, she sits up, throws out her arms in one last gesture of drama, and cries, 'See, *niña*, see – tonight I sleep in the bed of my *antepasados*, my ancestors!'

You shut the door on her hurriedly, desperate for sleep, and cross the terrace to your own room to prepare for the night before having to deal with the morning.

You are wrong. You are not done with her. You have undressed, climbed up into your own bed and are trying to still your mind, free it from all the incoherent talk and disturbance, clear for a night's sleep, when you hear the most shrill and penetrating screams emerge from the Trickster's room. You pull your pillow over your head to shut them out, but then hear a door being wrenched open violently and tell yourself someone has come to take care of her. The screaming and wailing, however, only grow wilder, more hysterical, and then someone is hammering on your own door and you must get up and open it, telling yourself she is in distress and needs help. You find her barefoot on the terrace, her hair crazily unkempt, her beautiful clothes dishevelled, her eyes starting out of her head as she screams: '*Fantasmas! Espectros!* In my room! *He* sent them! Look, look, they have scratched me, they have bitten me, can you see? Help me, *niña*, save me, *niña*! The devil is here, he will kill me!'

You try to put your arms around her but she flings you off and throws herself onto the paving stones where she rolls, howling. What are you to do? You stand wringing your hands when Arturo appears, in dressing gown and slippers, to grapple with her, hauling her to her feet.

'What shall we do?' you cry. Ghosts, spectres – what has she got into her head now? That head, a teeming pit of fantasies. You feel yourself attacked, scratched, bitten too. You would not be surprised to see blood and look towards Arturo for help.

'Perhaps it will be better for her to sleep in another room,' he says, a desperate edge to the voice that had been so controlled, so suave. 'As you see, she is sick.' In between gasps as he keeps a tight hold of her, he asks, 'Do you mind changing rooms with her? Tomorrow I will send her back to San Miguel. They know her there, they know us, they will take care of her. Do you think you can go to La Manzanilla alone? I will instruct the taxi driver where to take you, I know someone who has rooms to let. I will telephone in advance. But now—' He is panting as he half leads, half drags his aunt into your room, beads of sweat on his forehead while she continues to throw herself about wildly in fear and distress, then collapses sobbing onto his shoulders. You have never seen a face so ravaged as hers in the dim light of the lantern.

You hurriedly collect your belongings, clear out of

the room so he can bring her in and cross over to hers as fast as you can. She – or her ghosts – have created chaos here – the bedclothes thrown onto the floor, the mosquito net torn down, a carafe of water knocked over, her own clothes strewn everywhere, and you are too tired to deal with it. You curl up miserable, frightened, on a small brocade-covered couch and leave her to Arturo, to their ancestors and their ancestors' ghosts, wait for morning to come and free you from them.

Only when Arturo shuts the taxi door, waves you off, then turns on his heel and disappears quickly into his haunted palazzo, do you remember that you had not asked him the one question you had for him, the one you had come to ask: had Mother visited him once, on *her* way to La Manzanilla?

In sick disappointment you slouch back into your seat and try to close your eyes and ears to the whole debacle and let the heat, the thick odours of the small taxi and the pounding music being played on its radio, as well as the effects of the sleepless night, overtake you. But the light pouring out of the cloudless sky forces your eyes to stay open and face the fact: if the ghosts and spectres that the Trickster claimed had attacked her had proven to have their roots in the realities of her ancestry, then Rosarita the

Artist might also have been conjured out of a fragment of truth – a chance encounter with a stranger in the Jardín, a charmed moment embroidered by recollection. For the Trickster the two waters met and melded, the resulting murk was her natural element; she floated in it, swam.

It was you who would not allow them to combine, struggled to keep them separate in order not to drown. What if you too allowed them to merge and become one?

You cover your eyes with your arm and beg sleep to draw down its curtain.

V

A change in the air wakes you. It has become warm, humid, lifting off the ocean which is still invisible as you descend from the forested hills and gorges of Colima in rapid swoops and swerves, but there is no mistaking its closeness when you turn off the highway onto a flat sandy plain, dried grasses standing in what must once have been marshes, now drained. An egret takes off from a still, reflective pool, trailing its legs like afterthoughts, and you feel it lift you with it into the hazy light. Palm trees appear and cast little shade on rooftops of tin or thatch and verandas where people sit dozing and rocking. Coconuts are being sold on roadside stalls, and immense bottles of orangeade and Coca-Cola. Then there are more houses, built more closely together along the road, taller and larger, painted and tiled, with wrought-iron or metal sheet gates and bougainvillea flowering along the walls. There are shops for car and bicycle parts and hardware, taco and torta stands. Sleeping dogs stir in their beds of dust and some rouse themselves to chase your taxi for a bit but soon fall back and settle down to scratching at fleas. Schoolchildren on their way home from school, carrying heavy backpacks that make them stoop like old workmen, wait to cross the road. Some wave, some call.

You sit up and take it all in and ask the driver Pedro how much further you need to go. He replies with only an airy wave of the hand that he is dangling out of an open window, clearly enjoying the warmth, the sea air, and advising you to relax and do the same.

Then you are driving down what is obviously the main street of the town, lined with shops and businesses that declare their goods and services – a pharmacy, a café, a tourist office advertising whale-watching tours and mangrove trips – then into an empty plaza with a few benches, a few palm trees and at one end a church built of cement and painted red and white. Nothing historic, nothing in the least imposing.

From there the taxi swerves onto a narrow dirt road running alongside a canal. Here it stops. You peer down at its reeds, its surface of bubbling algae and look at Pedro in enquiry. He has lifted out your bag, opened your door and beckons you to follow him across a small wooden bridge. There is no sign for a hotel or lodging house but you have no option but to follow where he goes.

And then, there is the ocean. The Pacific. You have seen the Indian Ocean from Pondicherry, the Arabian Sea from Goa, but the opening out, through a grove of palms, onto the sands of La Manzanilla and the perfect arc of La Tenacatita bay lights you up with a blaze of joy such as you had thought you would never again experience. You want to throw out your arms, run like a bird across the sand, cry out with relief, the relief that feels like joy. You have arrived, and in one instant you have recovered what you thought was lost: clarity, clarity, the promise of clarity.

Pedro looks back at you laughing as he plods through the sand with your bag towards the forested cliff that bounds one arm of the bay, then down an avenue of palms that line a path across a green lawn to a long, low white bungalow at the foot of the cliff. Here he deposits your bag, smiles over one last transaction, the payment, and leaves you to yourself.

That is sobering.

★

Apart from the sound of the waves rushing in, crashing into the rocks below the garden and withdrawing with a long sigh, there is no other sound, and the house seems uninhabited. But once you climb the steps up to the veranda, wondering how to make your presence known and to whom, you see there is a table and some chairs at one end and two men bending over some work they are doing together. They pay you no attention. The table is covered with sheets of paper, pots of paint, jars full of brushes and many plain clay jars and platters which they are painting with great absorption. One is a stooped elderly man with sparse white hair, his lower half clothed in loose cotton shorts, his upper in loose brown wrinkles. The other is young, slim, dark, wearing the barest sketch of swimming trunks. He rises and bends over the old man to comment on something in the painting he is doing on a clay platter.

You decide it is up to you to make yourself known, and cough and ask, 'Ehh – is the owner . . . ?' making them look in your direction at last. The young man smiles a greeting but the old man frowns and, raising one bristling eyebrow, says drily in heavily accented English, 'Another visiting artist?'

'No,' you say, very loudly and positively. 'I am a visitor but not an artist – *at all.*'

The men lose interest and return to their painting but someone in the house has heard you; a door opens and a man steps out who seems to be in charge, possibly the owner. He is very large, very tanned, dressed in a Hawaiian shirt patterned with palm leaves and parrots over his khaki shorts and for some reason, perhaps his size, you take him for a Texan. 'Arturo rang,' he tells you, 'said you wanted a room for a bit. Come along,' and takes you into what appears to be his office. There are no signs of art on his desk although the walls are hung with the work of, presumably, the artists who have been here – various, simple, mediocre. After he has entered your name in a ledger, he offers to show you your room and carries your bag into it. You follow.

The room you have been allotted is at the very end of the veranda, which ends in a tangle of vines around a balustrade looking out over the furthest arm of the beach where a few brown pelicans are rocking sedately as grandmothers on the waves. The room is spare with only the most necessary bits of furniture but out on the veranda there is a hammock and geckoes peering inquisitively out of the tiles that make up the roof.

'Will do?' the Texan asks and smiles widely at the enthusiasm with which you nod. It will, it certainly will.

He puts your bag down and leaves, smiling as though this was exactly what he had expected. You pull off your sandals, enter the small bathroom behind a plastic curtain to wash at a basin lined with shells and return to stretch out on the hard, narrow bed. It is all you want.

When you wake from your daytime sleep the light at the small barred window is more shadow than light. How long have you slept? You rise hurriedly, open the door and survey the scene before you. It is the moment when the perfect circle of the sun begins to collapse: the top flattens, the centre bellies out like an orange rotting, and the weight of it drags it down so the sea, darkening, can rise up and swallow it whole in an instant so swift you almost miss it.

But you have not and the drama of it is so perfectly orchestrated you feel like applauding as you might the successful end of a performance. Of course you do not but you distinctly hear clapping and shouts of 'Bravo!' So you look down the length of the veranda to where the sound came from and see a woman sprawled on top of the step leading down to the lawn. She lifts the glass in her hand sloshing with ice, and laughs. The young man you had seen earlier is leaning over the balustrade, also with a glass in his hand, tinkling, laughing along with her, and he too exclaims 'Bravo!' Only the old man remains seated at the table, his head sunken between his shoulders, an aged turtle looking at nothing.

Before you can step back into your room, they have seen you and call, 'Come, come have a drink. Meet Bertha,' and there is nothing for it but to do so. Bertha is blonde, her hair the colour of corn, the rest of her as brown and wrinkled as a twist of ginger root. She wears a faded flowered cotton dress that she has gathered up between her legs, her large knees rise on either side and her feet are bare on the sandy stone steps. You are not sure if you are expected to sit down at the table or beside her when she flings out an arm towards you, so you go and stand next to the young man whose name you learn is Valentine. 'And our Sheppy.' She introduces you to the third in the party in a louder voice, suggesting he is a bit deaf. 'Don't forget our dear Sheppy. Sheppy? Is he asleep?' He grunts to deny it. Valentine pours you a drink you had not asked for but now you toy with it, enjoying the shape of the goblet, the beads of moisture slipping down its sides.

A door further down the veranda opens and the owner comes out with a bowl full of fresh coconut. He introduces himself now as Bruce, offering you some. His geniality has not waned with the day. You can see this group will form every evening to celebrate the sunset, and stay talking on the veranda till the sky is dark enough for the stars to come out. Bertha confirms that when she tells you she comes every evening for a drink with them. She shares a house with a group of friends. 'Girlfriends. You'll have to meet them. We haven't met anyone new for so long. Come sit with me, tell me your name, tell me who you are.'

Their friendliness is so open, so guileless, offered with open hands: why do you shrink? You had expected to be alone with the ocean and the evening but you cannot hold their presence against them.

Down on the beach, amongst the palm leaves, lanterns have been lit at Bar Bambu and music is playing. This is not a place you might encounter a ghost. Did you expect to, want to?

In the morning, when you emerge from your first swim in the Pacific, its salt bubbles sliding off you, you hear that cheerful call: 'Hull-o-oo! Come join us, honey!' There they all are, the girlfriends, and you pull your smock over your head and plod through the sand to meet them, gathered under a striped umbrella. They want you to have a beer with them, you ask for fresh coconut juice and smile and smile as hard as you can while Bertha presents you as a visitor from India. 'India! India!' the name has its usual uninformed, ecstatic response. 'Oh, I've always wanted to go! I'm waiting to be invited to an Indian wedding,' and, 'Please, please get married and invite me!' Another comes up with yoga, asks if you will give her lessons. You have never had a lesson yourself, nor are you planning to marry.

'But perhaps you have come here to paint?' suggests Françoise of the dark glasses and the dark drawl.

'No, no, she ought to *be* painted. Oh, if our artist Fabrizio sees you, he will ask you to model,' they all agree. 'He hasn't asked any of *us*,' they add.

You are frantic to divert the conversation from art, artists, maestros. Should you return to the sea for another swim, submerge yourself in another element? You know Mother would never have been part of their circle, her ghost would not come up in their midst. And when you begin to listen again, they have moved on and are telling their stories of other exotic people they have come across, and it is not necessary to contribute, to compete; what exotica can you find for them in family life and studies?

'But you are travelling alone? Why? Where are you planning to go? Or perhaps you'll stay?'

What answer can you give? You have none.

'Stay, do!' They give you all the reasons you should – the most beautiful bay in the world where you could see whales sporting, the sun hot and bright every single day, the restaurants along the beach serving the freshest fish . . . but can these really be the reasons they stayed, you wonder. They begin to divulge other reasons why they turned their backs on the worlds of their past – but it is clear they all know each other's stories, there is little left to tell, so they circle back to yours which is intriguingly empty and incomplete. 'There's a captain whose wife is dead, he lives all alone in that palazzo he's built on the hill. He *is* older than you, of course, but *still* . . . and the artist you must meet, but he doesn't come down to the beach often . . . and oh, why don't we all go to El Tamarindo or El Careyes for an expensive weekend, swim in a *swimming* pool, not this scummy sea, and watch to see who has come in on those luxury cruise ships from Puerto Vallarta, you'd surely catch *their* eyes, millionaires, divorcés . . .'

The more they talk, the less you listen, and finally the noonday heat makes everyone begin to nod, shuffle on their sandals and make their way to the beach shacks for a beer, a bite, a siesta, and you can slip away in the opposite direction, cross the bridge over the stagnant canal where a solitary heron stands vigilant, and walk down sleepy after-noon lanes.

In a bower of coconut palms, agaves and flowering

hibiscus, you glimpse the tiled roof of what might be the artist's studio because there is a slight, silent man in a straw hat meditatively raking the sand of a path through it as if he were painting it: could you go up and ask him if he had ever met someone who might have been your mother? In a brief, hallucinatory moment you see her turning onto that path, walking up it, entering that painting and vanishing into it.

For that one moment, it is so real that you are paralysed, and wait there for her to come out, then break away in a panic for fear she might.

Days that you keep to the bungalow, seated at your end of the veranda, looking out over a tangle of vines at the glittering bay beyond, listening to the waves approach then retreat and, as the heat grows, the dry rasping of cicadas, the sound of silence itself. A very long, slim and black iguana watches you from the vines with a fixed eye. It hypnotizes you and perhaps you hypnotize it; both of you remain stock-still under the sun that throbs in the cloudless, unblemished sky where frigate birds are wheeling above the fishermen who stand waist-deep, silhouetted against the pale sea under the pale sky with their fishing nets, immobilized with attention.

Valentine alone remains immune to the silence, the stillness. He comes by from the table at the end where art is being made, to show you a clay pot to which shells have been stuck 'by Sheppy', he tells you, although Sheppy himself seems sunk in his usual gloom. Unaffected by it, Valentine picks up his surfboard and strides out to the beach with it and flings himself with a shout of joy into the waves that come rushing to meet him.

Early that morning he had called out to you to come and join him and Bruce to see a mother whale and her infant who had swum into the bay to gambol. You had sat on the balustrade in your pyjamas, looking out at the pearlescent sea under a sky still tinted pink with dawn, and watched two rounded grey bubbles rising up out of the water and then diving back into it till the sun grew too bright and too hot and the pair drifted back towards the open ocean. For the rest of the day you had returned again and again to that image and in all the heat and brightness it had made you shiver as at an apparition.

The town itself is free of ghosts, of phantoms. It is small, you quickly learn it – with relief at being free to do it on your own, with no Trickster to intervene and intrude. When you sit on a bench in the small plaza before the modest church, both devoid of the glamour of the

Jardín and the Parroquia of historic San Miguel, you are grateful for its spare, bright starkness and the small lives you are allowed to observe as calmly as in a dream or at the cinema.

The bells ring at unexpected times and once you see a young woman come riding up on a bicycle, dismount and seize a string dangling from the belfry to give it a pull that makes a sound like a tin pot being struck. Old women in trim aprons come up carrying stalks of gladioli nearly as tall as themselves into the church. On a weekend there might be a wedding or a confirmation; both involve youngsters, boys in their best suits and their hair greased, their shoes shining, girls in white frocks and ribbons, holding flowers and pirouetting, elders stiff and grey with pride, lined up on the steps for a photograph. One group of ten- and twelve-year-old boys comes tearing across the plaza on rusty, clanking bicycles, ringing their bells and shouting 'Ma-ra-do-na! Ma-ra-do-na!' and are followed by a young mother pushing a strawberry-pink pram with a frilly pink umbrella and under it a little girl holding a pink plastic doll, then, as if this were a miniature parade, vanishing down a sandy lane. When they are gone a white rabbit timidly appears, perhaps a fugitive from the veterinary clinic at the corner; then it too is gone.

Now the plaza is empty, the stage waits for the next act. Who will appear now, you wonder, certain that someone will – but who will it be, Mother or Trickster? Or are they after all the same?

You walk down the full length of the short main street so often that you learn all its *negocios*, even the people who run them and those who use them. There is the *farmacia* where the pharmacist sits rocking, with one foot, the cradle in which her grandchild lies asleep while overseeing the older ones' homework and chatting with friends who drop in, breaking off now and then to give someone an injection or bandage the foot of a fisherman who has cut it open on a rusty chain. There is the ecological tour office where a young man who sits under a poster of a rainbow-coloured sunset reflected in a sea smiles and waves at you and tries once again to entice you into a whale-watching boat ride in the bay or a canoe ride through a mangrove swamp to see egrets nesting. In the pie shop there is always someone coming by to see if there is a fish pie that day or else a shepherd's pie to take home; above it the pieman's wife sits on a rocking chair on her balcony, surveying the scene below as calmly as a pelican on the waves in the bay. Flocks of schoolchildren crowd into the stationery store, then disperse, twittering, with their purchases. Posters of a coming rodeo are being pasted onto lamp posts and walls. A pack of stray dogs races through the street searching for a brawl, an adventure. Periodically the truck delivering gas cylinders goes by, blowing a horn that sounds like the bellow of a gored bull, and makes every dog in the vicinity sit up and howl. Or a truck might come by from the country with a harvest of melons and cucumbers that makes housewives come out of their kitchens to buy. Another pack of stray dogs goes racing by on its inscrutable business, stopping now and then to brawl ferociously over a bitch or a bone, making furious pedestrians step out of their way.

The street comes to an end behind a hardware store and a fish taco stand, at the edge of the mangrove swamp where marsh crocodiles pile up on one another, as still as stone, as baleful as idols, half-submerged in duckweed and algae; they might be dead if it were not for the half-raised lids over their watchful eyes.

If you dare walk past these grim gatekeepers, you come out where the last of the beach houses lie hidden in coconut tree groves. This is not the tourist season: most of them are boarded up and vacant, waiting for owners who occupy them seasonally. In the few that still are occupied, preparations are going on for the evening – children playing in outdoor showers, bathing, changing, while parents are preparing dinner on outdoor grills and dogs are barking but less aggressively now, more calmly, conversationally, quite outdone by the shrieks of homecoming parrots.

You take to the beach again to see how low the evening sun has dipped; and let the incoming waves rush up to your feet, then fall back in a frothy murmur. You stoop to pick up a starfish already so dead as to have turned into a shell, and upright one that is still alive and waving its floral tendrils in distress so it may meet the next wave and return to its aquatic element. Flocks of stiff-legged sandpipers are racing ahead of you in search, always in search. Small crabs are scuttling before them.

As the tide is rising to its highest level you clamber up the dunes spread with vines that bear flat mauve flowers by day that will be dead by night. At the top the slant rays of the sinking sun light up a whitewashed cross draped with susurrating paper flowers. There is a path beside it that leads into the cemetery and you take it so you may once again before you leave wander around the graves dug deep into the sand. Some have sunk so low they have disappeared into it, just the crosses raising their splintered arms to mark them. A few have been kept freshly whitewashed and have bougainvillea with papery pink and white flowers planted around them. Here must fishermen and boat-builders be buried, priests and toddy brewers, parents and children and grandparents: the history of the town itself. You try to decipher names and dates on the tablets that are still faintly legible.

Why? What makes you imagine you will come upon one with her name, her dates on it, black on white in drifting sand? She did not die here. When she died you were not with her. It was your sister Indu who saw to her cremation as she had to Father's, and who sent a terse letter to describe it to you in a flat, unemotional report that did not accuse you of being absent but left you feeling accused. Their assets had been disposed of and your share was, with incontrovertible fairness, at your disposal now. Just as you had shed her, she implied, she now shed you. Go free.

Leaving the cemetery behind you, you come out to sit on the dunes, sifting sand through your fingers, separating small shells from it. The sun is dropping rapidly now to meet the sea, that daily mystery of the merging of fire and water, light and dark. It is clear that one day the sea will rise and reach the cemetery, flood it and drown the graves, the ones so prettily decorated and tended and the ones neglected and forgotten. Perhaps the coffins will be dislodged and the receding tide will float them out towards the ocean like so many boats after a storm. When the tide turns, will they then return to land or sink and never be seen again?

You stay, pondering the question as you collect a handful of shells, shake them free of sand and toss them out to sea; the remains.

You have come as far as you can, you tell yourself: you can go no further.

Author's Note

When the Partition of India took place in 1947, trains carried untold numbers of refugees across the new borders of India and Pakistan, which bears some resemblances to the historical role played by trains in the Mexican Revolution of the 1910s, carrying both the militia and the revolutionaries. Violence and bloodshed accompanied both these events on a horrific scale.

★

The GI Bill passed by the US Congress in 1944 made free university education available to returning war veterans. Some of them went to Mexico, a few to study art in San Miguel de Allende.

Quite unusually, there was also one Indian artist, Satish Gujral, who came on a scholarship to study mural art and clearly saw the parallel between the Mexican Revolution and India's Partition that, as a refugee, he had experienced himself. His paintings are filled with the same violence and tragedy as the murals of his maestros, Diego Rivera and David Alfaro Siqueiros.